End Goal

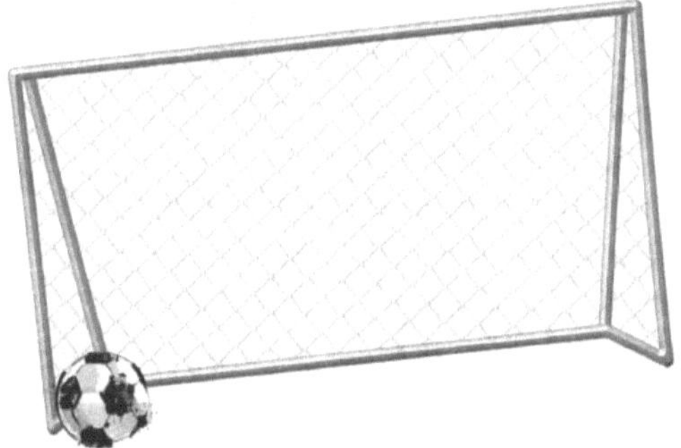

A Harris Brother Scottish Wedding

AMY DAWS

Copyright © 2018 Amy Daws

All rights reserved.

Published by: Amy Daws, LLC
ISBN 13: 978-1-944565-15-2
ISBN 10: 1-944565-15-9
Editing: Stephanie Rose
Formatting: Amy Daws
Cover Design: Amy Daws
Cover Photography: Dan Thorson
Cover Model: Adam Spahn

CHAPTER 1
Cocky Teammates

Camden

"Specs!" I shout as I jog across the grass toward my fiancée. She's in the middle of the Tower Park pitch surrounded by a sea of balls and has her hands all over my brother Booker.

Normally, my woman's hands on another bloke would send me into a jealous rage. But Specs—aka Dr. Indie Porter—is the assistant team doctor for Bethnal Green F.C., so I kind of have to deal with it.

Bethnal is the football club—or soccer team, as Americans call it—my dad, Vaughn Harris, manages in London. It's where my younger brother, Booker, and my twin brother, Tanner, play. Last year, I was right beside them until I signed on with Arsenal. Our older brother, Gareth, plays defence for Manchester United. We're a family of footballers through and through. And even though our sister, Vi, doesn't play, she's the loudest fan you'll hear in the stands at any of our matches.

Needless to say, we all eat, sleep, and breathe football.

That's why I thought my life was over when I tore my ACL last year. I was caked in mud from a rainy match when they wheeled me into The Royal London Hospital on a stretcher. With my football career at risk, I was feeling the lowest I'd ever felt.

Then a stunning, curly-haired redhead with cheetah-print glasses and a sexy smart mouth waltzed into the exam room, claiming to be a doctor. I thought she was way too young and gorgeous to be a doctor, but it turned out she was my surgeon and a brilliant one at that.

She is way too good for me, which is exactly why I put a ring on her finger several months ago.

"Oi! Get your hands off my brother, you slapper!" I crow as I kick a few stray balls out of the way and reach Indie, who's hunched over as she stretches out Booker's hamstring. I rear back my hand and slap my fiancée's arse with a satisfying crack.

"Ouch, Camden!" Indie squeals. Her hands immediately drop Booker's leg and fly back to rub her rear end. She turns wide, angry eyes at me that are framed by a pair of red glasses today. "What on earth are you doing? This is my place of work! You can't come in here and do that!"

I roll my eyes at her overreaction. I grew up on this pitch. This is where I learned the game of football. There's absolutely nothing I could do here that would shock anyone.

I wrap my arm around Indie and pull her to my side. "Relax, Specs. When your dad manages the team, no one blinks an eye at you." I release my hold on her to bend over and pick up one of the many footballs spread out all around us. Moving away, I begin bouncing it on my knees and head nod to Booker, who's still lying on the grass. "Hey, Book."

"Cam," Booker replies, pulling his knee to his chest to stretch himself like he was perfectly capable of doing all along. The cheeky wanker.

I glance over at my beautiful fiancée, who is currently shooting daggers at me. Her brown eyes are stunning as ever, but they do not look soothed by my words. "I'm serious, Cam. You can't come around the pitch to see me whenever you feel like it."

I stop bouncing the ball and clutch it to my hip. "Why not?"

"Because it's unprofessional."

"Stuff that! You've broken the rules for me before," I reply with a wink. Memories of Indie playing hot doctor and me being the naughty patient will be the highlight of my life when my balls are old and saggy. Forbidden romances always do taste the sweetest.

"Well, no more," she retorts firmly. "I don't need anyone else talking crap about me because I'm engaged to the manager's son." She closes her eyes and grimaces like she didn't mean to say the last part.

I drop the ball and turn to my brother. "Who is talking crap?"

Booker rises up to a sitting position and props his arms on his knees. "Tanner and I put them straight. Don't worry about it, Cam."

"Tell me," I nearly growl and kick the football high, toward the goal that's over half a football field away. It bounces off the top bar and misses.

Out of nowhere, Tanner leaps up onto my tensed back. His beard tickles the side of my face as he bellows, "Hey, broseph! What are you doing here? Did the Gunners fire you already?"

He tries to pull me in a headlock, but I shove him off and kick another football in frustration. "No…I'm already done for the day. What's this shit I'm hearing about the team trash-talking Indie?"

"Camden!" Indie exclaims, attempting to grab my arm and pull me toward her. "Just leave it. I've got it handled."

Tanner's eyes narrow as he crosses his arms and stares back at me. It's hard to take him seriously with his man bun and Dumbledore beard. However, he's lost all humour on his face, so I know this isn't a laughing matter.

"I've had words with them," he states with a grim tone that's very unlike him.

"Words with who?" I ask through clenched teeth. I rear back to kick another football. This one makes it in the net easily. "What are they saying?"

Out of the corner of my eye, I see Booker shake his head at Tanner.

My blood pressure spikes. "What are you guys not telling me? I want to hear it all."

Tanner exhales heavily. "We have to tell him, Book."

Booker winces and yanks off his goalie gloves before hopping up to his feet. "I overheard some of the guys saying that you only put a ring on Indie's finger as a publicity stunt for your new team."

"What?" I roar, my hands raking through my hair. I clench the locks tightly in my fists because I'd rather be punching their faces. A lot of the guys used to be my teammates. Who the fuck would say that?

"Guys, stop!" Indie exclaims, trying to stand between the three of us to halt our conversation, but we've essentially boxed her out. This is a brother moment that can't be interrupted. If Gareth were here, he'd be initiating a Harris Shakedown.

Tanner looks straight at me and replies, "They were saying you don't have any intention of marrying her. They were even saying the ring is a fake."

"My fists of fury are going to fucking fly!" My face heats with rage as I spin on my heel and boot four balls in a row. Three of the four hit the goal. The last one buzzes way over the top bar because I scooped under it too much.

My eyes dart all over the pitch to where the rest of the players are making their way toward the changing room on the opposite side. I begin walking. "Time for me to have words with some of my former teammates."

"We handled it, broseph," Tanner barks, grabbing hold of my arms and yanking me backward. "Trust me. Booker and I both got fined for *handling* it."

Indie rushes up in front of me and pushes my chest. "Camden, you're only going to make it worse!"

Her voice breaks on the end with barely contained emotion. It's then that my rage is tempered. Snuffed out. Crushed by the woman I'm in love with. I look down into Indie's glossy eyes and it fucking guts me.

"Indie, they are saying I don't want to marry you because we haven't set a date," I grind out through clenched teeth though I hardly need to spell it out for her. She's the smartest person I know. "There are two ways we can fix this. Either you set the date already, or I punch their fucking lights out."

Indie's face crumples in worry as she nervously gnaws on her lower lip. Her anxiety kills me because she has all the power here. I wanted to get married right away, but she was the one dragging her bloody feet.

My jaw is tight when I plead with her one more time. "Specs, just set a bloody date already."

She turns away from me and begins hurriedly picking up stray footballs. Months. It's been months that my brilliant fiancée has avoided this conversation with me and I'm tired of it.

With a heavy sigh, I turn back to Booker and Tanner. "Tell me what your fines were so I can pay you back. You guys don't have to fight my battles for me."

"Fuck off," Tanner growls while tightening his hair-band. "We're Harris Brothers and Indie is our friend. This is as much our fight as it is yours."

Booker nods in agreement and they both cross their arms over their chests, clearly setting their decision in stone. After a moment of staring at them, I finally nod a silent thanks and they give me a hearty pat on the back before making their way off the pitch.

Indie is still completely focused on placing the stray balls into the sack, clearly trying to avoid talking to me.

I stride over and bend to grab a ball. "Is this a typical job for the team doctor?"

"No," she snaps quickly, then adjusts her glasses as they slip down her nose.

"Specs." I state her nickname softly and walk toward her as she bends to pick up another ball. "Specs," I repeat as she fumbles to drop the ball inside with only one hand.

The bag falls to the ground, several footballs spilling out around our feet. I reach up and grasp her cheeks in my hands to force her to look at me. Her eyes swerve nervously all around as she checks for people who may be watching us.

"Camden, please," she croaks, her voice thick with emotion as she tries to pull out of my embrace.

"No," I reply, moving my hands from her face and wrapping them around her waist to hug her to me.

Indie has never been huge on affection, but she's changed with me. When we're together at our house in Notting Hill, she's completely open. Right now, she's reminding me of the closed off surgeon who was raised by cold, unfeeling parents who left her alone in boarding schools for most of her life.

"Indie, I love you. Fucking marry me so we can put this stupid gossip to bed."

Her eyes fly wide. "I'm not going to marry you because a couple of guys don't know how to keep their mouths shut in the changing room!" she snaps.

"Then marry me because I asked you to. Marry me because I want to take the next step with you!"

"And who will attend this wedding?" she asks, stepping out of my arms and swiping under her glasses as errant tears fall from her eyes. "Your entire family and my one and only friend, Belle? Not to mention the fact that Belle is married to Tanner, so she's technically your family!"

"So what! Who cares who we invite? Everyone loves you."

"My parents don't even send me birthday cards anymore. You think they're going to attend their only daughter's wedding? Highly doubtful."

My heart plummets when the truth comes out at last. Indie has been pushing off on setting a wedding date because of her horrid parents.

"We don't need your parents there," I reply through clenched teeth. "Truth be told, I don't even want them there."

"Who will walk me down the aisle?" she sobs, and the pain on her face cuts right through me. In a flash, I kick all the balls out of my way and pull her into my arms.

She presses her face into my chest as her body trembles against me. I haven't seen her get emotional about her parents in a long time. I'm such a prat for not realising this is what has been bothering her.

"Any of my brothers would love to walk you down the aisle. You can take your pick." I run my hand down the back of her neck and she sags into me a bit. "I know my dad would be honoured, Specs. Hell, I'll walk you down the aisle myself if you'll let me."

"I'm sorry, Camden," she mumbles against my shirt before looking up at me, her brown eyes full of pain and embarrassment. "This is so stupid. I shouldn't care about this, but I do. I don't want to be the bride everyone feels sorry for because there's only one friend on her side of the church."

"So let's get married alone!" I reply, my voice rising in pitch.

She scoffs and shoves me in the chest. "Be serious. Your family would murder you."

"I don't give a toss!" I tilt her chin up so she looks me in the eyes and sees how serious I am. "I care about you and me. My family will get over it. Most of them at least. Tanner will probably weep for a few weeks, but he'll be fine."

Indie smiles at the image and shakes her head from side-to-side. "We can't possibly elope, can we?" she asks, her voice sounding mildly hopeful.

"We can do whatever we want!" I exclaim, tossing my hands out wide. "Let's do it this weekend. We're both off, which basically never happens in the world of football. It's a sign, Specs. It's meant to be."

Indie bites her lip and adjusts her glasses, clearly thinking through all the details like the sexy nerdling she is. "Are you completely sure you're okay with it just being us? I don't want you to do this because of what the players are saying, and I don't want you to have regrets."

"I'm one hundred percent sure I want to marry you this weekend…Just us," I add, stepping in and hugging her to me again. I press my forehead to hers and whisper, "Let's go make those cocky bastards shut their arrogant mouths."

CHAPTER 2
Cocky Bagpiper

Indie

"The piper's ready for ye!" the wedding planner states in a thick Scottish accent as I stare at myself in the mirror of the hotel lobby in Gretna Green, Scotland.

I'm wearing a simple pleated, strapless wedding dress. The ivory colour compliments my fair skin, and the skirt is just full enough to make it feel like a wedding dress. The sweetheart neckline gives it a sexier feel while the row of buttons up the back adds a touch of elegance. No accessories and definitely no glasses. I can't wait for Camden to see me.

We only had three days to prepare everything, and doing it all without his family finding out was incredibly difficult. Those five Harris siblings are balls-deep in each other's lives. His sister called three times when we were on the train yesterday. Even my best friend, Belle, nearly figured things out when she caught me shopping in our old neighbourhood in East London a couple days ago. It's been a whirlwind!

But Cam has always loved a *challenge*.

Now we're here, at the Gardens Hotel in Gretna Green—a village in southern Scotland, over the border of England. It's famous for runaway weddings, dating back to the 1800s. Young lovers would cross the border to defy their families and get married in secret, which is perfect for what Cam and I are doing.

The Harris family is going to flip when they find out what we've done, but I couldn't be happier right now. From the exciting train ride, to arriving at the station, to a limo escort, everything has clicked into place. The wedding planner took care of all the details, including separate hotel rooms for the night before. It was important to me to have some traditional aspects in our elopement. I didn't want to lose all the elements of a normal wedding just because it was a spur-of-the-moment decision.

At our romantic dinner the night before, I swear you couldn't wipe the smiles off our faces because we knew what we were about to do. Not even rain on my wedding day will bring me down.

I move through the lobby to the rear exit that leads to a stunning garden filled with perfectly manicured hedges and a giant Japanese red maple tree. Drops of rain glisten on the petals of purple heather blooms that head toward a small pond where Camden awaits.

"Whenever yer ready," the wedding planner says, handing me an open umbrella. "Good luck."

She moves back as I tuck myself underneath and step out into the light mist. An elderly man strides up from behind her, wearing a traditional Scottish kilt and carrying enormous bagpipes in his arms.

He smiles a crooked-tooth smile and says in his thick accent, "They say rain on yer wedding day means good luck for fertility." He shoots me a lewd wink and I can't help but laugh.

"That's good to know."

"Are ye ready, lass?" he asks, putting the reed of his instrument in his mouth.

I clutch my bouquet of pink roses and give him a quick nod. "Completely ready."

And just like that, I'm walking through a beautiful—albeit wet—Scottish garden with a traditional Scottish bagpiper leading me down the aisle.

When I carefully cross over a stunning, red-railing arched bridge, I finally see my future husband standing tall and proud under the rustic pagoda.

Camden is, of course, kitted out in a kilt himself. It was a bit of a shock when he said he wanted to wear one. But when the wedding planner showed him the tartan for the Harris name and he nearly wept with joy, I couldn't say no.

God, he actually looks sexy. The knee-high socks are exactly like the ones he wears on the football pitch, and the suit jacket is tailored to his build perfectly. What can I say? I like my man in a skirt!

My focus on him is diverted when the bagpiper in front of me trips over a stone. He belts out a cringe-worthy, nasally note as he tumbles to the ground, landing hard on his elbow. Without pause, I rush over to him and drop my umbrella on the ground.

"Are you all right?" I ask, squinting through the rain and placing my free hand on his ankle.

The Scotsman's eyes go wide. "Yer hair, lass. Yer dress!" He nearly drops the bagpipes as he grabs the umbrella to hold over my head from his position on the ground.

"It's fine," I state, pushing my long red hair back behind my shoulders. The hairdresser spent hours taming my mane into perfectly smooth tendrils, but I knew it would never last as soon as I saw the rain. *Curly hair problems.* "Are you hurt, though? It looked like you might have twisted your ankle. Stay still while I have a look."

His eyes are nearly hidden amongst the crinkles that take over his entire face. "Aye, I'm right as rain. Just an old geezer who cannae watch where he's walking." He wipes away the mud on his knee and smiles apologetically.

I smile and shake my head. "It must be difficult with that thing strapped to your front."

He nods and hands the umbrella back to me so he can stand. With great effort, he pushes up off the ground and readjusts the bagpipes over his chest. "Let's get ye married, aye? Or perhaps ye want tae ditch this wee lad and run away with me instead? I promise, I'm more agile than I look."

I erupt into laughter as the cocky bagpiper waggles his brows at me suggestively.

"Everyone okay?" Camden's voice pulls my attention away as I look over and see him approaching. He's left his position under the dry alter where we'll exchange our vows. Rain beads off his wool suit jacket and down his arms, but something about his blue eyes in the grey daylight is dreamy.

"We're fine," I reply with a laugh. "Although, it's good you've come. I think our proud piper here was just about to whisk me away to the Highlands."

Camden frowns at the old man, who doesn't look the least bit intimidated as he places the reed in his mouth and begins playing again with an extra flourish and more eyebrow waggles.

Cam turns back to me in confusion. "I think I should walk you the rest of the way. I don't trust the twinkle in that bloke's eyes."

With a huge smile, I reach out and grab his hand, pulling him under the umbrella with me. "Sounds perfect."

He smiles down at my rain-drizzled face, his own just as damp as his smoothed back hair. When his body presses up against mine, I instantly wish we were done with the wedding part and in our honeymoon cottage.

"It's strange to see you without your glasses, Specs," Camden murmurs softly, a wicked glint in his eyes.

"It's strange to see you wearing a skirt, Camden," I retort, glancing down and taking in his suit jacket, vest, and red tartan tie that matches his kilt.

"It's called a kilt. It's very manly," he corrects with a tight jaw. "And just wait 'til you see what's underneath. That's definitely manly."

I can't help but giggle and roll my eyes—a very familiar response when it comes to my future husband. He drops a kiss on my forehead, then pulls back to look at my full body.

"If I were smarter, I would have let you struggle a bit longer in the rain."

"Why is that?" I ask, my brows knitting together as I look down at my dress that has a good inch of mud on the hemline.

"Because your dress is white." He waggles his brows and glances down at my chest with a lascivious smirk.

"You're cockier than the bagpiper I think," I murmur under my breath and jab him in the ribs with my bouquet.

"And you're the most beautiful woman I've ever laid eyes on," he replies quickly, his face losing all humour as he stares straight into my soul.

My kneejerk reaction is to complain about my ruined hair or my runny makeup, or maybe whine about how I didn't have time to get my dress hemmed and now it's ruined by the rain. But I'm too happy to let all those thoughts cloud my mind. Today I'm marrying Camden Harris and nothing is going to get me down.

As we follow the bagpiper down the aisle, Camden holds the umbrella over us and leans down to whisper in my ear. "Hey, Specs, why does Snoop Dog need an umbrella?"

I look up at him curiously. "Why?"

"For drizzle."

Camden's pun causes a laugh to burst unexpectedly from my belly, and I think it caught the bagpiper off guard because he let one of those high notes slip again. Thankfully, he didn't trip.

We finally make our way up to the safety of the pagoda in one soggy piece. Our earlier teasing is forgotten when the registrar begins the service. Camden and I face each other, holding hands beneath the hanging glass lanterns that twinkle yellow lights all around us. A portable heater warms my bare arms and shoulders as I adjust my strapless dress. I wipe at some mud splatters on my skirt that only end up smearing, and I'm instantly transported back to the first time I met Camden.

He was covered in mud and laid out on a stretcher, playing the part of a cocky football player. But he wasn't only an athlete womaniser looking to have sex with his surgeon. He was a Harris Brother, which meant more than I ever could have ever realised on my own.

The registrar indicates it's time for us to say our vows to each other, and Camden is the one to go first.

"Indie Porter, I promise to love you more than cheesy puns, more than James Patterson novels, and more than football. I promise to pour you coffee every morning and let you spoon me every night without talking about it the next day. I promise to be understanding when you'd rather read a boring textbook than watch telly with me. And I promise to be fully supportive of your career in sports medicine, no matter how many blokes you have to put your hands on.

"You made me want more out of life, Specs. You saw so much more in me than just my family and football. You helped me see a life outside of my own little world. Because of that, for the rest of my life, everything I have is *thine*. All my possessions, my wisdom, my humour, my hopelessness and hope, my passion and, above all, my love is thine, as thou art mine."

Tears slide down my cheeks as he repeats the mantra that has become my most treasured words out of his mouth. He said them to me the first time we made love. Every time I hear them now, I remember exactly what made me fall in love with him.

The registrar gestures for me to begin, so I take a deep breath and steel myself to speak from the heart, which has never been as easy for me as it has been for Camden.

"Camden Harris, I had a list of qualities for the kind of man I wanted to marry. A description. A type. I had everything planned out. Then you happened." I pause and fail to wipe the smile off my face as I have flashbacks of Camden and his brothers barrelling into my hospital. "I had this person's character traits listed out in great detail, but the one thing that was never on my list was love. Love was a foreign concept to me because of how I grew up. That's why I appreciated my charts and checklists. They gave me a sense of purpose. But you were someone I never could have planned on because you don't belong on a list, Camden. You belong with me. You were meant for me, and I'm so grateful to take the Harris name today. I'm ready to be a part of a real, genuine family…with you. You are my family, Camden. You've shown me what love feels like. Because of that, I will be thine forever and always. Thank you so much for being inappropriate and kissing me in the hospital when you were my patient."

Camden laughs, his glossy eyes spilling tears down his face. "I believe it was you who kissed me in the surgical theatre later on."

I giggle. "We are full of inappropriate moments."

He nods proudly. "And now we'll have a lifetime to make more."

The registrar says a few more things I don't hear. But when he says we can kiss, he has my full attention.

Camden leans in, cups my face in his hands, and presses his lips to mine in the most tender, soul-affirming kiss of my entire life. It isn't a kiss of passion or lust, sex or attraction. It's a kiss that feels like home and a lifetime of promises to be there for each other, no matter what.

CHAPTER 3
Cock and Balls

Camden

It's dark out when I carry Indie through the rain, up to the entryway of the secluded stonewall honeymoon cottage that's been prepared for us. The building is tiny and located on the grounds of the majestic Caerlaverock Castle. It's apparently where the groundskeeper lived back in the 1800s, but the wedding planner said it is the most romantic place you can find near Gretna Green.

I finagle the door open and carry my giggling bride across the threshold into a stunning one-room cottage, covered in pink flower petals and illuminated by the fireplace and dozens of votive candles. The cottage looks like it was plucked straight out of some historic Scottish Highlands magazine. Indie slips out of my arms and gasps as she takes in the untainted character of a cottage that's easily two hundred years old. The original stone walls and cedar-plank flooring coupled with the roaring fire, plush rugs, and cosy furniture transform this piece of ancient history into a hideaway you never want to leave.

"Will this work okay for you, Mrs. Harris?" I ask, loosening my tie and following her as she makes her way over to the fire crackling in the stone hearth.

She smiles at my reference to her new last name. "It's a dream, Mr. Harris," she replies, her eyes trailing from the exposed beams on the ceiling to the giant four-post bed in the middle of the room. "This entire trip has been a dream. I'm so happy, I could burst."

Her curvy silhouette is outlined by the golden flames of the fire, and I can't help but think how fucking lucky I am to call her my wife. She's not just beautiful. She's intelligent, and quirky, and fun. She's everything. And the image of having little ginger-haired babies with her cleverness makes my chest ache with a desire that's stronger than I've ever felt before.

"I'm happy, too," I reply, draping my damp jacket over the sofa and stepping up behind her. I rest my chin on her shoulder and wrap my arms around her waist as we both gaze into the fire. "And I'm so glad that it was just the two of us today."

"Are you really?" she asks, her tone hesitant. "Are you sure you're not disappointed your family wasn't here? I mean, this wedding was kind of a mess with the rain and everything. Maybe something in London with your family would have been a bit more proper."

"Indie," I chastise softly and drop a kiss on her bare shoulder. "This wedding was us. Nothing about our relationship has ever been proper. Bloody hell, we started off under the guidance of a penis list for fuck's sake."

She giggles and covers her face with her hands. "Don't remind me."

With a proud grin, I turn her around to face me, my hands tightening around her waist as I pull her flush against my body. "I love my family, but I love us even more. Today was everything I hoped for."

Indie smiles and exhales heavily as she wraps her hands around my neck. Her brown eyes look thoughtfully up at me. "Very well then. But now that I'm a Harris, I intend to behave like one, which means I'll start inserting myself into everyone's business."

My chest vibrates with a silent laugh. "Is that how you see my family?"

She nods stoically. "Pretty much. Overbearing and over-caring. But I can survive it, especially since your brother married my best friend. Belle and I have great plans for you Harris twins."

"Oh?" I ask, arching a brow and squeezing her to me. Impatience rolls through my body as I realise we're both wearing way too many clothes in this honeymoon cottage. "Are you going to let me and Tanner in on our future plans that you have so clearly mapped out already?"

She shrugs and begins fiddling with the buttons on my shirt. "Well, obviously we're going go on holidays together."

"Obviously," I state, biting my lip and watching her focus intently on the task of removing my shirt.

"And eventually we'll want to move out of London to get away from the noise and the traffic. Something a bit quieter, possibly near your dad."

"Is that right?" I ask, my hands roaming up and down her ribcage as she yanks the tails of my shirt out from under my kilt.

"Of course we'll be neighbours with Belle and Tanner because we don't just want Harris Sunday dinners, but Friday Tequila Sunrise nights and Saturday morning English breakfasts while our kids play in the garden as well."

"Kids?" I ask with a laugh, completely captivated by this rant Indie is on and never wanting it to stop.

Indie frowns petulantly and pushes the shirt off my shoulders. She licks her lips and runs her hands down my bare chest and abs. I groan from the feeling of my cock growing hard beneath the tartan pleats.

"Of course," Indie replies, looking up at me and combing her fingers through my damp hair. "Our children will be best friends with Tanner and Belle's kids, and we'll want to live near the rest of your family so the cousins can remain close."

"Naturally," I add, biting my lip and reaching around to her back. My fingers find the long row of buttons down her spine, and I quickly begin sliding them through the loops. I lean in and murmur into her ear, "And how many children do you see for us, Mrs. Harris?"

"Oh, at least four."

I can hear her smiling. "Really? Just four?"

"Mmhmm. I'll still want to work, but I won't be travelling with a football team once I start having children. I imagine I'll open up my own athletic training centre that specialises in injury prevention. It will be revolutionary, of course."

"Of course," I murmur as her dress slides down her breasts. I push it over her hips, and it pools on the floor around her feet. She steps out of it, kicking the fabric off to the side so she stands before me in nothing but her white heels, her white strapless bra, and white knickers. My virgin bride.

Not quite, but she is one hundred percent mine, and there's a carnal part of me that loves the fact that she's never felt another man inside of her. I was her first. My seed is the only seed to have entered her body, and the thought of making babies with her has me hard as stone beneath my kilt.

My fingers reach back for her bra clasp. "What are your plans for me?" I whisper, kissing her earlobe and nuzzling into her scent.

She sucks in a sharp breath when her bra tumbles to the floor. I pull back to gaze down at her pale pink nipples, hard and pointing straight at me. I lean down and drop soft kisses on the mounds of her breasts.

"You'll retire eventually." She lets out a soft cry when I pull her tiny bud into my mouth. "And have loads of investments, so you won't have to work if you don't want to."

"That's good to hear," I reply, smiling as I suckle her other nipple and pull it hard and long between my lips.

"Oh God, but you'll bore easily," she moans. "You'll most likely start coaching our kids' football teams or helping out at Bethnal Green."

"That's very logical." I reach out to grab her hand and place it on my groin to show her the effect her words have on me. She bites her lip and wraps her fingers around me, letting out a tiny sigh of appreciation.

"You never asked me what I was wearing under my kilt, Specs," I murmur in a deep, wicked tone.

"I can already guess," she husks, swallowing and slowly slipping her hand up under the fabric. She grabs my bare shaft and smiles with glee. "Just as I suspected. Cock and balls."

I laugh at her cheekiness, and it takes everything I have not to rip her knickers off and fuck her senseless. This is our wedding night. It needs to be about more than uncontrolled lust.

I clear my throat and concentrate on the words I want to say next. "Are there any other plans you want to inform me about?" I ask as I slide my hand down the front of her knickers and gently tease the crease of her pussy.

She whimpers when I find her clit and apply delectable pressure. Her whimper changes to a full-on moan when I plunge a finger deep into her tight, wet centre. "We can alternate hosting Christmas and other holidays," she cries.

I grin and continue plunging into her. "You know, for a bird who likes her space, you sure have concocted quite a plan to keep everyone close."

She opens her brown eyes to me. They are filled with something meaningful and important. Something that I want to remember forever. "It's because I'm madly in love with you, Camden, and you've completely changed me."

My chest soars with pride from her words. In a flash, I lose the battle to take this slow and yank her knickers off, along with the rest of my getup. I lay her down on the plush fur rug in front of the fire and gaze down at our naked bodies as her legs wrap around my waist.

The head of my cock teases her opening and she pumps her greedy hips up toward me. "I love you, too, Indie," I reply, pushing her hair back from her face and staring deep into her eyes.

With one meaningful look, I thrust deeply into her. As deep as I can reach. As deep as she can take me. I let my weight sink down on top of her so my body consumes her. So I can feel every breath she takes and every moan she utters.

My jaw is tight as I pull back and stroke my cock inside of her, building speed with each and every pump. The fire heats my skin and the rug sticks to my palms, but the silkiness of Indie's skin against mine is perfection.

Her hands run over my face, my shoulders, my arms, and my back. Her moaning grows louder and more frenzied as she reaches around to grab my arse. She pulls me tight against her, holding me inside her as she tenses. I hold my breath and watch in wonder as her orgasm detonates through her entire body, vibrating in her chest, then her stomach, through her thighs, and finally clamping down on my cock inside of her.

I feel it all. Her orgasm. Her desire. Her passion. Her love.

When her eyes open and look up at me, I can see it all. Our future. Our plans. Our family. Our life.

Once her climax descends and her body relaxes, she lifts her head and grabs my face to kiss me. Her tongue dives hot and wet into my mouth, and it's all the touch I need to fall over the edge as well.

Our mouths break apart, but I'm still inside of her, pulsing and groaning as I empty everything I have into my wife.

My life.

My Indie.

CHAPTER 4
Cocky Homecoming

Camden

We're back in London just in time for the weekly Harris Sunday dinner. Indie and I can't stop smiling the entire drive out to Dad's house. As far as weddings go, there is no way any couple in the whole world could have enjoyed themselves more than we did in Scotland.

When we walk in through the kitchen, I see my family out back in the garden. Tanner, Booker, and Gareth are doting over our niece, Rocky, who's playing with a football in the grass while Booker's pregnant girlfriend, Poppy, sits at the nearby picnic table with Dad, Belle, Vi, and Vi's fiancé, Hayden. Everyone is here. Everyone is always here. Harris Sunday dinners are sacred. They are the one constant we all have regardless of how busy we are or how much our family is changing. And seeing the huge changes that have been happening as of late, I'm certain that our news won't be that big of a surprise.

Vi sees us come out back and gives us a jovial wave. "Hiya, guys."

Everyone looks at us expectantly, as if they instinctually know we have something to share.

"You're pregnant," Tanner bellows, shaking his head knowingly.

"I'm not pregnant," I reply, rolling my eyes at him.

He rolls his eyes right back at me. "I mean Indie's pregnant."

"She's not pregnant," I retort, quietly adding, "Yet."

"What?" Vi asks, her brows furrowed in confusion.

I inhale a deep breath. "Well, first comes love…Then comes marriage."

"You got married?" Vi squeals, shooting up from the table.

I nod. "We eloped this weekend. I'd like to introduce you all to the new Mrs. Indie Harris."

My family erupts into cheers and they all rush over and sweep us into one big hug. Even my brother Gareth, who has been a moody sod for months now, seems genuinely happy for us. I look around and wonder why Tanner hasn't lifted me over his shoulders like the mental patient he is. It's then that I see him standing on the outside of our hug, his arms crossed over his chest with a pouty scowl on his face.

Booker rolls his eyes and attempts to yank Tanner into the group, but Tanner resists. I move past Indie, but Tanner turns his back on me when he sees me approaching and loudly says, "Booker, would you tell Camden that I'm not speaking to him?"

Booker frowns at me and replies, "He's standing right here and can clearly hear you, so no, I'm not telling him that."

Tanner narrows his eyes at our youngest brother and shoves him hard in the shoulder. He re-crosses his arms and juts his chin up into the air. "Would you tell him that he had a lot of nerve getting engaged without telling me first, but to go off and get married without me by his side is total bollocks and completely unforgivable."

Tanner's voice breaks on the last word, and I have to cover my mouth to stop myself from bursting into laughter. Indie winces at his reaction, but I place a reassuring hand on her arms to soothe her.

"Tanner, come on now. It was an important decision for us." I move to grab his shoulder, but he recoils away from me.

"Tell my former twin brother that I won't speak to him for the rest of my life." Tanner's voice wobbles as he crosses his arms and turns his back on me again.

"Tanner!" I shout his name in frustration. "We had our reasons."

"I don't care!" he bellows and Belle strides over shaking her head at him.

She hits him with a dark, warning stare. "You're being ridiculous."

"Wife!" Tanner exclaims, dropping his arms and stomping his foot like a petulant child. "You're supposed to be on my side."

"No," she retorts. "You're being obnoxious. Our best friends just got married. We should be happy for them or at least fake it until our egos recover."

With a heavy sigh, Tanner turns and looks at me, shaking his head gloomily. I move in and wrap my arms around his shoulders, squeezing him tight to me. "I only married Indie so quickly because now we can have our babies together, bro."

His eyes fly wide. "What?" he exclaims. "What are you talking about?"

"Ask Belle what she and Indie have planned for our futures and tell me it doesn't sound brilliant. We can start our families together, Tan."

Tanner looks at Belle with childlike excitement spread all over his face. "Our kids can be best mates and learn how to play with balls together like we did!"

I nod knowingly. "And play football together."

"This changes everything!" Tanner bellows, clapping his hands together in anticipation.

Belle shakes her head. "You are aware that medically there's a high probability that Indie and I won't conceive in the exact same month. Who knows what our fertility cycles are like. Not to mention, I'm a bit older than Indie, so my egg quality is slightly lower."

"Oh, Wife," Tanner cuts her off with a hearty slap on her arse. "Would you stop being a doctor for one minute and just dream with us?"

"Yeah," I add, pulling my bride under my arm. "Besides, Harris Brothers have super sperm. If we will them, they will come."

Tanner hoots with laughter and high-fives me. "Classic pun, bro!"

"And not at all cocky," Indie says with a great big smile meant just for me.

THE END

Check out Camden and Indie's full-length story:
Challenge

And sign up for my newsletter to be notified of my latest book news.
www.AmyDawsAuthor.com

MORE BOOKS BY AMY DAWS

The Harris Brothers Series:
British Sports Romance
Challenge: Camden's Story
Endurance: Tanner's Story
Keeper: Booker's Story
Surrender & Dominate: Gareth's Duet, Coming Soon

Wait With Me: Romantic Comedy Standalone

The London Lovers Series:
Becoming Us: Finley's Story Part 1
A Broken Us: Finley's Story Part 2
London Bound: Leslie's Story
Not The One: Reyna's Story
That One Moment: Hayden & Vi's Story
One Wild Night: Julie's Story, Coming Soon

Pointe of Breaking: Amy Daws & Sarah J. Pepper

Chasing Hope: A Mother's *True* Story of Loss, Heartbreak, and the Miracle of Hope

For all retailer purchase links, visit:
www.amydawsauthor.com

MORE ABOUT THE AUTHOR

Amy Daws is an Amazon Top 25 bestselling author of sexy, contemporary romance novels. She enjoys writing love stories that take place in America, as well as across the pond in England; especially about those footy-playing Harris Brothers of hers. When Amy is not writing in a tire shop waiting room, she's watching Gilmore Girls, or singing karaoke in the living room with her daughter while Daddy smiles awkwardly from a distance.

For more of Amy's work, visit: www.amydawsauthor.com or check out the links below.

www.facebook.com/amydawsauthor
www.twitter.com/amydawsauthor
instagram.com/amydawsauthor

www.ingramcontent.com/pod-product-compliance
Lightning Source LLC
Chambersburg PA
CBHW051830180726
48283CB00004BA/1378